MICHAELA MORGAN

Illustrated by Dee Shulman

OXFORD
UNIVERSITY PRESS

OXFORD
UNIVERSITY PRESS

Great Clarendon Street, Oxford OX2 6DP

Oxford University Press is a department of the University of Oxford.
It furthers the University's objective of excellence in research, scholarship,
and education by publishing worldwide in

Oxford   New York
Auckland   Cape Town   Dar es Salaam   Hong Kong   Karachi
Kuala Lumpur   Madrid   Melbourne   Mexico City   Nairobi
New Delhi   Shanghai   Taipei   Toronto

With offices in
Argentina   Austria   Brazil   Chile   Czech Republic   France   Greece
Guatemala   Hungary   Italy   Japan   Poland   Portugal   Singapore
South Korea   Switzerland   Thailand   Turkey   Ukraine   Vietnam

Oxford is a registered trade mark of Oxford University Press
in the UK and in certain other countries

British Library Cataloguing in Publication Data
Data available

ISBN-13: 978-0-19-919997-6
ISBN-10: 0-19-919997-3

1 3 5 7 9 10 8 6 4 2

Available in packs
Stage 12 More Stories C Pack of 6:
ISBN-13: 978-0-19-919991-4; ISBN-10: 0-19-919991-4
Stage 12 More Stories C Class Pack:
ISBN-13: 978-0-19-919998-3; ISBN-10: 0-19-919998-1
Guided Reading Cards also available:
ISBN-13: 978-0-19-918375-3; ISBN-10: 0-19-918375-9

Cover artwork by Dee Schulman
Photograph of Michaela Morgan © Richard Drewe

Printed by Ashford Colour Press

Chapter 1

Shelley Holmes was *bored* again.

So was her best friend, Kelly

and so was Dustbin, her dog.

sigh

It was the middle of the long holidays.

There were weeks more of…

...nothing to do.

They were all watching an old video and wishing.

Then Shelley had one
of her ideas.

5

'I bet WE could do that!' she said.

'I'm not swinging on
a trapeze or walking
on a high wire,' said Kelly,
'or juggling fire or
having knives thrown
at me!'

'I mean I bet
we could train
animals,' said
Shelley.
'**I** could do it!
I could be a
world famous
animal trainer.'

I'd wear feathers
in my hair...
high heels...
sparkly tights.
I can see it now...
my name in lights.'

SHELLEY HOLMES
☆ WORLD FAMOUS ☆
ANIMAL TRAINER

'Hmm…' said Kelly.

ZZZZ said Dustbin.

'It will be EASY
PEASY,' said
Shelley.

'It can't be that hard.
How hard can it be to
make a pony run in
a ring

or a chimp wear a hat…

or get an
elephant to stand
on three legs?

We could do that, no problem!
No problem at all.'

Kelly thought about it for a bit.
Then she said, 'Well, we do have one
problem...'

'Hmm...'
said Shelley.

Dustbin woke up.

Chapter 2

Shelley and Kelly dragged Dustbin down to see their friend, the vet.

'We want to learn how to train Dustbin,' said Shelley.

'That's a GOOD idea,' said the vet.

'You could train him to stop eating my waiting room.'

'Now let me see... There are lots of different sorts of training.'

She gave them some leaflets.

SMART
HEART
AGILITY
TRAINING

Has your dog
got the heart
of an athlete?

Come along to our
weekly sessions
at: 118 High Jump
Pounding

SHEEP
DOG
TRAINING
Sheep Farm
Sheep Wash

FLYBALL
A new
playful
training

Fun fitness for
dogs!
Bounce Lane

OBEDIENCE
TRAINING

Teach your
dog to obey
your every
command.

Sportshall
2 Stern Road

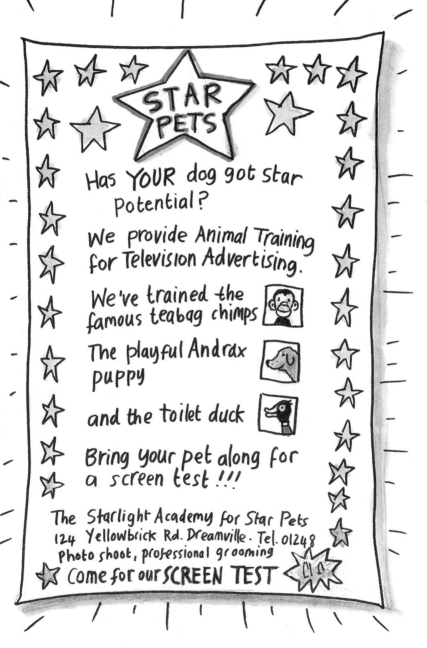

13

'That's the one for us!' said Shelley. 'I want to train Dustbin up to be a star. And I'll become a world famous animal trainer.'

But then the vet pointed out some of the more important details on the leaflets.

So they decided to go for the
Obedience Training in the Sports
Centre.

'It's a start,'
said Shelley.
'Come on,
Dustbin.
You'll love it!'

Chapter 3

The Sports Centre was very busy.
There was Fun and Fitness for the
Over-40s.

There was a disco upstairs.

There was swimming in the pool.

The Brownies' Tea Party was in the small hall,

and in the big hall... dog training.

There were dogs of all shapes and sizes all waiting for a chance to show how obedient they were.

Some of them were old friends.

There was Colin the collie and his owner.

There was Fifi the poodle and her owner.

There was Bully the bulldog and his owner and Spotty the Dalmatian and his owner and... rather a lot of others.

YAP! YAP!

RUFF

They had all been before
– except Dustbin.

They were all eager to trot to heel
– except Dustbin.

Dustbin!

They were all waiting quietly
– except Dustbin.

'Let's go,' hissed Kelly. 'Dustbin can't do any of this.'

But Shelley was determined.

'Keep your dogs on their leads,' said the teacher, 'and reward him or her with regular treats – a bit of sausage, a biscuit, a doggy chocolate drop...'

All the owners had come
prepared with smart leads,

special chains,

whistles
and clickers,

pockets full of
treats,

and lots of spare
treats which they kept
in bags around the hall.

Shelley and Kelly were not quite so well prepared.

Dustbin's lead was slightly chewed, and they hadn't thought about bringing any doggy treats.

'I've got some raspberry bubble gum,' whispered Kelly. 'We could try that.'

'We'll start with something very easy,' said the teacher.

Walking forward ... Normal pace... Start now!

All the dogs trotted off
smartly and earned praise

Good dog!

Oos a ickle
tweasure then?

and treats.

But Dustbin
was less
than keen.

What? No
choccy drops!

All the other dogs were given treats.
But not Dustbin.

'When he does as
he's told he gets a
treat. And not
before!' said the
teacher.

Humph!

Now about turn.
Normal pace.
Walk back.

All the dogs turned around smartly and walked back sensibly.

But not Dustbin. He was more interested in treats.

So he didn't get a reward, and Shelley was not pleased.

How is a person supposed to become a World famous animal trainer with an animal like this?

The next thing the
owners and dogs were
asked to do was...
weaving.

What?!

'Take your dog, on its lead, and
weave in and out of the others. Go!'
Most of the dogs were quite
good at this,

but not Dustbin.

So Dustbin still got no treats,
and he was getting quite hungry.

'I think Dustbin is
a bit peckish,' Kelly
whispered.

Peckish?
I'm famished.

27

'He'll be good at the next thing,' said
Shelley. But he wasn't.

He didn't get a treat for walking to
heel.

He didn't get a treat for sitting

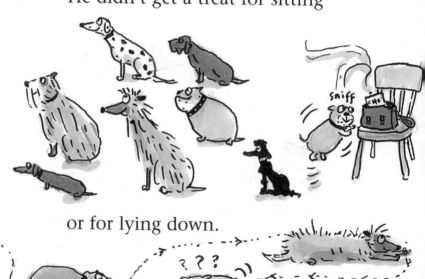

or for lying down.

Dustbin was one disappointed dog and Shelley was one unhappy animal trainer. 'I can't be expected to become a world famous animal trainer working with Dustbin. He's hopeless!'

By the end of the session Shelley and Dustbin were getting desperate

and when the teacher said, 'We will now let each dog off the lead for the recall exercise,' Kelly had a feeling that all would not go well.

'Let's get out of here,' Kelly hissed.
But Shelley was determined.

I can make him do it! I know I can!

Shelley took Dustbin off his lead and Kelly held him, tightly, while Shelley walked to the other end of the hall.

'When I give the order,' said the teacher looking at Kelly, 'you release the dog.

Then,' and here she looked at Shelley, 'you give the recall signal.'

'Then the dog,' and here she glared at Dustbin, 'the dog will run straight to you and sit by your side.'

The teacher gave her commands.

First to Kelly:

Then to Shelley:

Then to Dustbin:

Dustbin went.
He went like the wind.

He went into the corner to snaffle the sausages.

He went through everyone's pockets trawling for treats.

He went into bags and boxes chomping the chocolate drops and then...
he kept going.

He went into the small hall to join
in the Brownies' tea

Slobber!

and he even went upstairs to the
disco...

where he ate
the snacks,

drank the
drinks

and even danced
a couple of
dances.

'I refuse to have that dog in this class,' said the teacher.

'He'll have to go down into the puppy class.'

'Sorry,' said Shelley.

'Sorry,' said Kelly.

'Perhaps this isn't the sort of training for us. We'll try somewhere else... sorry...'

Sorry.

Sorry.

Chapter 3

Dustbin looked downhearted.

And so did Shelley. 'I give up,' she sighed. 'I'll never be able to train him.'

'I suppose... we could try... the agility training,' Kelly suggested.

'**YES!**' said Shelley. 'Dustbin will be great at that. And it **is** the cheapest. This is the way to our fame and fortune!'

Kelly was not so sure.

She was even less sure when she heard what Dustbin was expected to do.

'What the dogs do,' said the teacher, 'is simply climb these steps,

walk this plank,

jump over this fence,

go through this tunnel,

over the see-saw and through the hoop.'

What?

How?

Why?

'And when they get to the end we give them a treat.'

Oh, now I see!

Dustbin did his best.

He walked the plank,

AAAH!

jumped the fence   sort of,

went through the tunnel,

over the see-saw,

oops!

and through
the hoop.

'Now he deserves a reward,' said the teacher.

'So... we pat his head and tell him he's a good boy!'

After that Dustbin went on strike.

Even Shelley was fed
up with the training.

So was Kelly

and … so was Dustbin

'Maybe I won't be a world famous
animal trainer after all,' Shelley
was thinking. 'Maybe I'll be
something more
sensible, like …'

But then Shelley heard something very interesting…

Chapter 4

Kelly managed to get Dustbin's name on the register.

Shelley had very high hopes.

Kelly had very deep doubts

and Dustbin had … a very rumbly tummy.

The afternoon was spent
grooming the dogs
for stardom.

They were all

bathed,

brushed,

fluffed up

and smoothed down.

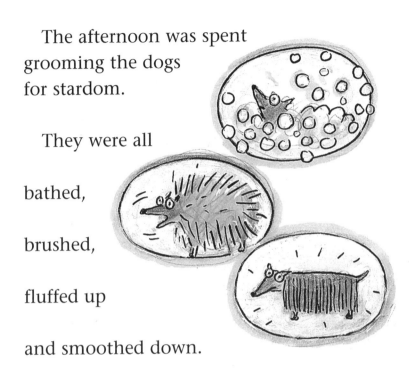

In the end they were all sweet-
smelling, glossy-coated and smart –
well, nearly all.

Shelley and Kelly did their best with
Dustbin but it wasn't easy.

He'd eaten his brush.

BURP!

Soon Mr Beilsperg, the film producer, and his team arrived to put the dogs through their paces and to choose the

 new star for the Krunchkins dog food ad. The dogs and their owners lined up for the first test.

This was the beauty competition.

'We want to select a good-looking dog,' said the film producer.

'Hmm- not bad...'

'Very shiny coat.'

'Great teeth.'

'Bright eyes!'

'Mmm... of course looks aren't everything!'

The next test was the fitness test.

The next test was the intelligence test.

'For this test your dog has to get to the box, press the pad, release the ball, catch it and bring it back.

O.K. Go!'

Dustbin did his best.

At least he got to eat the ball.

'Dustbin has no chance. Let's get out of here,' said Kelly.

But there was one last test.

'This is the most important test of all... and the easiest,' said Mr Beilsperg.

'We simply pour out a bowl of delicious Krunchkins and we film your dogs eating it and looking happy.'

The film producer poured
out the Krunchkins.

It looked like
sawdust with a few
beans and peas thrown in.

Bully's owner muttered:

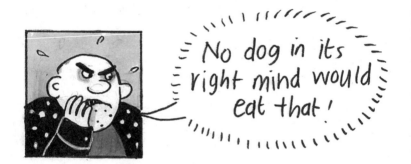

No dog in its right mind would eat that!

Fifi looked at it and sniffed.

No, No, zey cannot be serious!

Colin's collie wouldn't even go near it.

Bully looked at it and bit the hand that fed him.

'All the dogs have failed,' said the producer and his team...
and then they saw Dustbin.

First he nibbled,
thoughtfully.

Then he licked,
appreciatively.

Then he chewed –
thoroughly –

and then he
scoffed the lot
and beamed.

'That dog has a superb appetite!' said the producer.

'He's the one for us!'

HOORAY!

So all the next week Kelly, Shelley and Dustbin were treated like stars and Dustbin was given bowls and bowls and bowls

to eat and he ate every single one right down to the last dusty crumb.

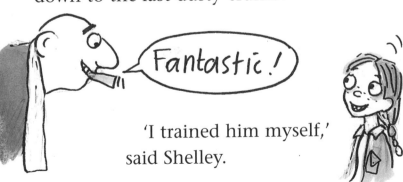

Fantastic!

'I trained him myself,' said Shelley.

By Friday, the filming was finished.

'That's it,' said Mr Beilsperg. 'The film is made! Thanks for everything. Now we have to do the testing for the toilet duck.'

Shelley was DELIGHTED.

'There!' she said to Kelly. 'I knew we could do it.'

But behind her,
Dustbin was just
finishing off another
tasty little snack.

BURP!

KRUNCHKINS
ADVERT
FINISHED FILM

Pardon me!

About the author

This is my second story
about Shelley, illustrated
by Dee Shulman.

I had a dog that was
very much like Dustbin.

He could eat anything (toys,
books, shoes, his own dog bowl).

He could jump in the air and twirl.

But he never learned to obey a simple
command like 'Stay!' or 'Sit!'

Perhaps I should have taken him
to dog school?